TEEN TITANS GO!™

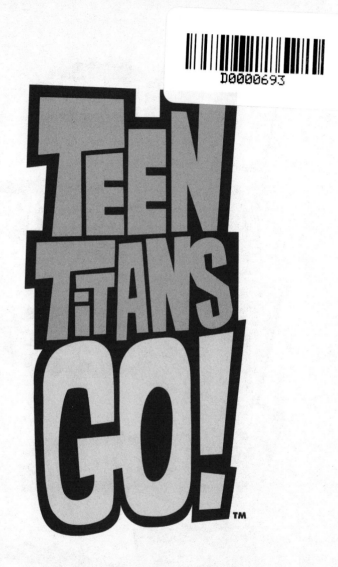

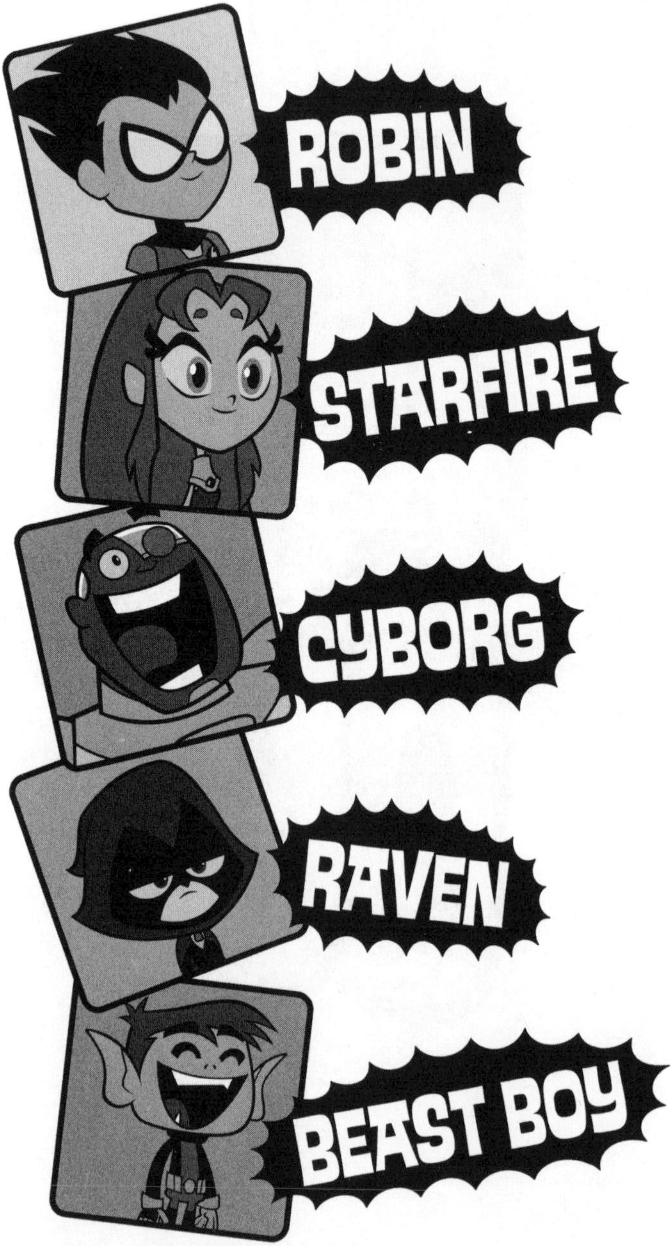
ROBIN
STARFIRE
CYBORG
RAVEN
BEAST BOY

STARFIRE STARBOMB

Adapted by **Steve Korté**
Based on the episodes
"**Blackfire Blow Up**" written by **John Loy**
"**Tamaranian Vacation**" written by **Amy Wolfram**
and
"**Knowledge**" by **Michael Jelenic**

LITTLE, BROWN AND COMPANY
New York   Boston

Little, Brown and Company

Hachette Book Group
1290 Avenue of the Americas, New York, NY 10104
Visit us at lb-kids.com

Little, Brown and Company is a division of Hachette Book Group, Inc.
The Little, Brown name and logo are trademarks of Hachette Book Group, Inc.

The publisher is not responsible for websites (or their content) that are not owned by the publisher.

First Edition: September 2016

ISBN 978-0-316-35645-9

Library of Congress Control Number: 2016939317

10 9 8 7 6 5 4 3 2 1

RRD-C

Printed in the United States of America

CONTENTS

BLACKFIRE BLOW UP

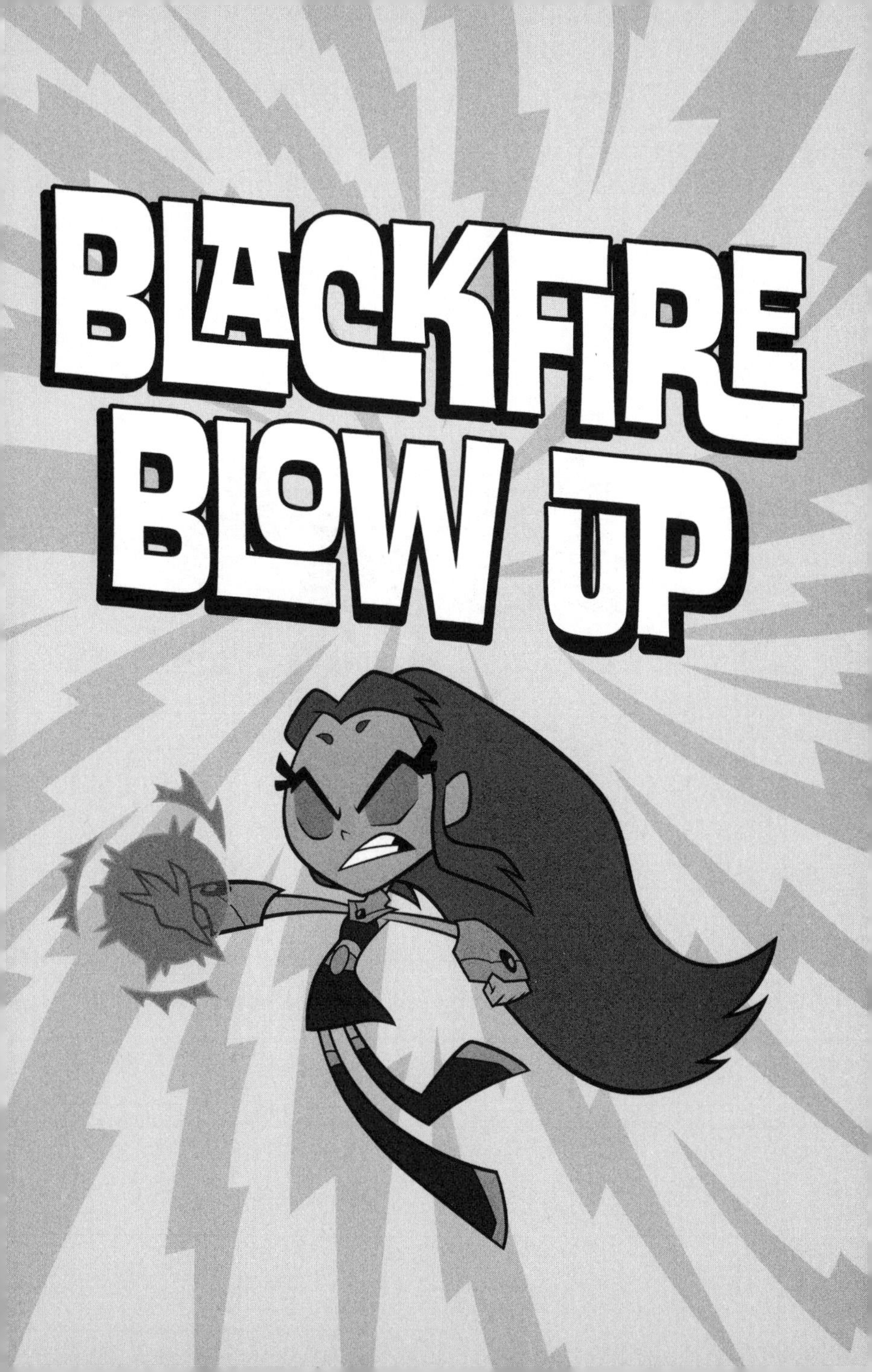

CHAPTER 1

It was an awesome summer day, perfect for planting flowers, and that's *just* what Starfire was doing.

"The flowers, the flowers grow in the ground," she sang. *"Give them the water, or they will die."*

The happiest member of the Teen Titans was floating above the lawn that surrounded Titans Tower, the team's headquarters, and singing as she sprinkled water on her petunias and pansies.

Starfire couldn't remember the last time she had been this happy. What could possibly spoil this perfect day?

Ker-Blam!

Just then, a giant metal prison-security robot crashed down from the sky and smashed into the middle of her garden, crushing every single flower. Starfire watched in astonishment as smoke billowed from the wreckage and her sister Blackfire stepped out from behind the robot.

"Blackfire?!" said Starfire with a gasp.

Zap!

Four more robots appeared above the sisters, and one of the robots fired a laser blast directly at Blackfire.

"Hey, little sister," said Blackfire as she did a quick somersault to avoid the laser. "Cover my flank, okay?"

"Of course," said Starfire.

The two sisters zoomed into the air and flew back to back, facing the robots that gathered around them.

Zap! Zap! Zap!

As the robots bombarded Starfire and Blackfire with more laser blasts, the sisters fought back as hard as they could, shooting eye blasts and pummeling the machines with strong punches.

Blam!

Another robot downed by one of Starfire's starbolts!

"Um, Blackfire, what are you doing here?" she asked.

Blackfire destroyed a robot with an energy blast called a blackbolt and replied, "I came to see you, sweetie!"

"But you *never* visit," protested Starfire. "I…I thought you did not like me."

Rip!

Blackfire threw another robot to the ground, snapped off its head, and tossed it aside.

"Oh, honey, where did you ever get that idea? *Cover me!*" she yelled just as a robot moved closer to her.

Starfire zapped the robot with her signature starbolt energy blasts, and the machine exploded in the sky.

"You never return my calls," said Starfire.

"Got a new number!" yelled Blackfire as she dodged another laser blast.

"When I was five, you stole my favorite dolly!"

"Just so I could have something that reminded me of you!"

Starfire smiled happily as she grabbed the final robot, slamming it into tiny pieces with her fist. She turned to her sister.

"So you really came back here just for me? There is no other reason?" she asked.

"I just had to see my baby sister," Blackfire said as the two girls floated down to the ground.

"Then you promise you will not disappoint me again?" asked Starfire.

"Promise!"

Starfire reached out to Blackfire and hugged her as hard as she could.

"Oooh…Then we can begin the closeness!" Starfire said.

"Um, that's enough closeness for now," Blackfire said with a frown. "Enough hugging."

CHAPTER 2

Inside Titans Tower, the other four members of the Teen Titans were chilling in the living room. Raven was reading a book, Robin was lifting weights, and Cyborg and Beast Boy were sitting on the couch playing rock-paper-scissors. Starfire bounded into the room. She usually looked happy, but today she seemed *especially* happy.

"Friends," she called out. "Look who has paid us the surprise visit!"

"Oooh, I love surprises," said Cyborg.

Blackfire stepped into the room next to her sister, raised her hand to greet the Titans, and said, "Hi, everybody."

Instantly, the smiles of the four Titans vanished.

"But not *this* surprise," muttered Cyborg.

"Ew, it's her," said Raven.

"Ugh," added Beast Boy.

Starfire reached over to hug her sister again and said, "Yes, the her, herself!"

Robin put down his weights and marched over to the sisters. Blackfire smiled at Robin and ran her finger across his chin.

"Hey, Robin," she purred. "Did you miss me?"

Robin glared at her and shouted, "Uh, no. Because you are *evil*, and I am only attracted to *niceness* and *sweetness* and *innocent things*… like a puppy with ears too big for his head!"

Robin quickly pulled Starfire away and said, "Star, can I talk to you in the kitchen for a minute?"

Starfire replied, "Of course. And when I

come back, we can continue with the sisterly hugging."

In the kitchen, Starfire could barely contain her excitement.

"Can you believe that Blackfire has come to see *me*? Is that not wonderful?" she said happily.

"*No!*" Robin said firmly. "And again, *no*! Every time you let her into your life, she *crushes* you!"

Starfire said, "I do not think so, but—"

Robin interrupted her to say, "*Yes*. And again, *yes*! She is one of the most wanted criminals in the galaxy!"

Cyborg, Beast Boy, and Raven came into the kitchen and joined the conversation.

"Girl, that girl is bad-girl news, girl!" cautioned Cyborg.

"She's up to something," said Raven.

"And *ugh*!" added Beast Boy.

Blam!

Starfire emitted an eye blast that sent the other four Titans spinning across the kitchen and crashing into the wall.

"*Stop* it!" she yelled. "All I have ever wished for is to have the sister relationship. And

Blackfire knows that if she lets me down again, it will break my heart. And the darkness will ooze from my broken heart, contaminating the river of my soul."

The four Titans watched with apprehension as an inky blackness descended upon the kitchen, leaving only Starfire visible within an aura of glowing purple energy.

"Um, Star…" Robin began.

"Do not interrupt!" said Starfire as a howling wind began to swirl through the kitchen. "If my sister disappoints me again, then I, filled with poison, will rain death and destruction upon all the creatures of the universe, starting with…"

Suddenly, Starfire's dark spell was broken when Blackfire flew into the kitchen and grabbed her sister's hand.

"Hey, sis," said Blackfire, "I have the *best* idea! Let's dye our hair so we can be twinsies."

Starfire clapped her hands in delight and said, "I always wanted to be the twinsies! Sister fun time!"

As the two sisters floated merrily out of the room together, the other Titans exchanged nervous glances.

CHAPTER 3

"SISTER FUN TIME!" Starfire screeched.
Ten minutes later, she was standing in front
of a mirror, admiring her newly colored black
hair, her newly thickened black eyelashes,
and her newly painted black fingernails.
Blackfire stood next to her, admiring Starfire's
makeover.

"Oooh!" Starfire said happily as she studied
her reflection.

"You look great, sweetie," said Blackfire. "But it's missing something...."

Starfire looked worried and asked, "What?! What is missing?!"

Blackfire snapped her fingers and said, "Oh, I know what it is. It's that purple outfit of yours. We need to change that."

Blackfire reached into a paper bag and said, "Oh, look! I just *happen* to have an extra one of my outfits here."

Seconds later, Starfire was modeling a black top and skirt with black boots.

"That's *such* a great look for you," Blackfire said admiringly.

Happy tears began to form in Starfire's eyes as she turned to her sister and said, "There is something of meaning I wish to relay to you. I have dreamed of this for so long...."

Blackfire held up a finger to her mouth and said, "Shhh. Can it wait? Why don't you move over there, next to the window?"

Starfire looked puzzled, but she obligingly moved closer to the window.

"Like this?" she asked.

"Perfect," said Blackfire. "That's her!" she shouted suddenly, pointing at Starfire. "That's Blackfire, the escaped con you're looking for!"

Smash!

Suddenly, a prison-security robot crashed through the window and encased Starfire within a laser-detention ray. Starfire was unable to break free as the robot pulled her closer.

Starfire looked at her sister and slowly shook her head with sadness. She was so disappointed that she didn't even struggle as the robot carried her through the broken window and soared into the sky.

Blackfire peeked through the window and then smiled.

"Bye-bye, *sweetie*!" she called out as the robot and her sister zoomed into outer space.

Hours later, the robot delivered Starfire to the Intergalactic Metahuman Penitentiary, a giant steel-coated asteroid that circled Neptune. The robot held Starfire within its laser-detention ray as they floated past dozens of prison cells that contained alien beings, many of them manacled to the walls of their prison.

Clang!

The robot tossed Starfire into a tiny cell and then slammed the heavy metal door shut behind her.

Starfire surveyed the grim stone walls that surrounded her and listened to the howling laughter of some of the other inmates. Her usually happy smile faded from her face, and she formed her hands into fists. As she pounded her fists against the walls of her cell, she angrily called out one name over and over.

"*Blackfire!*" she yelled.

Back at Titans Tower, Blackfire was happily lounging on a couch, flipping through the pages of a magazine. She looked up as the Titans approached her.

Robin paused to look around and asked,

"Wait, where is Starfire? *What did you do to her*?!"

Blackfire shrugged and turned back to her magazine.

"Titans!" yelled Robin. "Dig up the yard!"

Within minutes, the lawn outside Titans Tower was pockmarked with giant holes after the four Titans dug up the ground in search of Starfire.

Blackfire emerged from the Tower, yawned, and said, "Calm down. She's fine. She's in jail…serving out my sentence."

Cyborg looked shocked and yelled, "Get me a sweater—because that is so cold!"

Robin glared at Blackfire and said, "This is why you showed up in the first place!"

"She trusted you," Raven said angrily.

"Dibs on Star's room!" Beast Boy called out.

As the other Titans glared at Beast Boy, he said, "*What*? She's got the best room in the Tower. And she's got a bidet!"

"You are the worst sister in the world," Raven declared.

Blackfire rolled her eyes and replied, "I can't be *the* worst."

Robin moved closer to Blackfire and said, "I have two jobs in this world. One: Eradicate evil! And two: Protect the precious heart of Starfire!"

"Cut me some slack," said Blackfire. "No one ever taught me how to be a good sister."

Cyborg jumped closer to Blackfire, put one robotic hand on her shoulder, and said,

"Then get yourself a backpack and a spiral notebook and a number-two pencil and a pen and a juice box and some healthy snacks and an apple for your teacher, because...*we are going to take you to sister school!*"

Blackfire looked alarmed as Beast Boy grabbed her arm and pulled her into Titans Tower.

"Sister school, yo!" he called out happily.

CHAPTER 4

The Titans gathered in Beast Boy's bedroom. They surrounded Blackfire, who was staring at her cell phone, trying her best to ignore them.

"Lesson number one: listening," Cyborg said slowly. "Now listen. So I can teach you to listen."

"Uh-huh, whatever," Blackfire said as she texted.

Cyborg looked annoyed, but he continued. "The keys to active listening are eye contact and hand-holding. Allow me to demonstrate."

He then grasped Beast Boy's hand, looked deep into his teammate's eyes, and said soothingly, "Go on, Beast Boy. *I'm listening.*"

"My problem is that I'm just *too* sweet and funny," Beast Boy said sadly, tears welling in his eyes. "And girls take advantage of me."

Cyborg nodded sympathetically and said, "I hear your pain. You have to talk it out, so you can walk it out." He turned to Blackfire and said, "Now *you* try."

Blackfire rolled her eyes, sighed, and placed her cell phone in her pocket. Beast Boy reached out his hand to her, and she reluctantly touched it.

"Go on, Beast Boy," she muttered.

"Sometimes I think I'll never find love...." Beast Boy began.

Blackfire quickly withdrew her hand and shouted, "Shut *up*!"

Beast Boy scurried into the corner of the room and let out a quiet whimper.

Robin stepped forward and said, "Okay, lesson number two: hugging. Blackfire, I want you to hug Beast Boy."

Blackfire reluctantly walked over to Beast Boy, reached out her hands, and briefly touched Beast Boy's shoulders.

"Terrible effort!" said Robin. "Again. This time with Raven."

Blackfire reached around Raven for two seconds and then pulled her arms away.

"No, no, no!" yelled Robin. "Here, I'll show you myself."

Robin walked over to Blackfire and said, "Arms out wide! Come in tight, but not too tight! Back pats optional!"

Whap!

Blackfire smiled happily as she threw her arms tightly around Robin. She sighed with contentment as she continued to hug him.

"That's much, much better," Robin said. "Okay, let go."

"Oh, but this feels *so* good," Blackfire said as she held on tight.

"No, no!" Robin said nervously. "Wrong kind of hug. Separate! *Separate!*"

Robin finally pulled free, caught his breath, and then he said, "Okay, time for lesson number three: role-play! Titans, assemble your Starfire outfits!"

Blackfire watched as the Titans reached into backpacks and pulled out long, flowing magenta wigs and purple Starfire outfits.

Within seconds, each Titan was dressed more or less exactly like Starfire.

Beast Boy brushed aside the magenta locks from his face and spoke in a singsong voice to Blackfire, "Oh, sister, I am here to tell you how you have made me feel all these years."

Blackfire laughed and said, "You look ridiculous."

Beast Boy pouted, then yelled, "*You* look ridiculous!"

Robin quickly pulled Beast Boy away and whispered, "Stick to the script!"

Cyborg jumped in and said, "What Starfire meant to say is do not be a *glorpnurp*, friend."

"*Glorpnurp*?" said Blackfire sarcastically. "That's not even a *word*, genius!"

"Hey! Don't make me come over there!" Cyborg said angrily.

33

"I told you this wouldn't work," Raven muttered to Robin.

"Stay in character," Robin replied. "What the Starfires are trying to say is this: When you were in trouble, who did you turn to? When you were in—"

Blackfire interrupted Robin to say, "I'm going to stop you right there…and tell you that exactly zero people care."

Robin angrily pulled the magenta wig off

his head and yelled, "I have *no* idea how Starfire could still love you after all you've put her through!"

Suddenly, Blackfire looked confused. She turned to the other Titans and asked, "She *loves* me?"

"Probably the only person in the universe who does," Beast Boy said sulkily as the Titans started to walk out of the room.

Tears began to form in Blackfire's eyes as she remembered the time that she and Starfire were little girls and she had snatched Tina Tinkles, Starfire's very favorite doll, out of her hands. Starfire had only responded with a sad smile and a warm hug.

"Wait, don't go!" Blackfire called out. "I want to be a better sister!"

CHAPTER

5

Deep within the Intergalactic Meta-
human Penitentiary, Starfire relentlessly did
push-ups on the cold stone floor. She was
wearing an orange prison jumpsuit, with the
sleeves ripped off to show her bulging biceps.
The only time she paused from her exercise
regimen was to glare at the wall above her.
There, taped to the wall of her cell, was a
photo of her sister, Blackfire. Starfire had

used her eye blasts to etch dozens of angry words into the stone wall near the picture: TRAITOR! BAD SISTER! DO NOT TRUST! LIAR! NEVER AGAIN! NO MERCY!

Starfire jumped to her feet and put her face inches away from the photo on the wall.

"You have broken my heart, sister," she said angrily. "Now I will break *you*!"

Starfire then looked into a mirror and grabbed an electric shaver.

Bzzzzzz!

With a dozen quick moves, Starfire ran the clippers through her hair, buzzing off all her flowing locks. She smiled as she surveyed the stubble atop her head. She flexed her right bicep, admiring a large tattoo—it was her sister's face, with a red *X* slashed across it.

One month later, after a steady regimen of push-ups, pull-ups, and weightlifting, Starfire had bulked up. A lot.

Crash!

She dropped a pair of seventy-five-pound dumbbells to the floor of her cell and then moved closer to the photo of Blackfire. She quickly blasted the photo with eye blasts, burning the letter X on top of her face.

"Sister fun time," she said with an evil chuckle.

Ker-Blam!

Starfire slammed her fist against the photo and knocked a gaping hole in the wall of her prison.

As the piercing sound of sirens filled the air, Starfire crawled through the hole and emerged outside the prison. Soon, she was zooming through outer space, heading back to Earth.

CHAPTER

6

Back in the living room of Titans Tower, Blackfire's sister training was in full swing. The Titans were huddled together on the couch, and Raven giggled happily as Blackfire completed her makeover. After Blackfire applied lipstick for her, Raven smiled into a mirror and admired her bright red lips and luxuriantly long eyelashes.

"Yeah, looks good," Raven said happily.

Blackfire reached over to give Raven a big hug and said, "I'm so glad you like it!"

"Um, could you give *me* a makeover?" Beast Boy asked. "I hate my look."

Blackfire smiled in sympathy, took Beast Boy's hands in her own, and said, "I hear somebody who's not happy with himself, but who *should* be...because he's *great!*"

"Awwwww, thanks!" Beast Boy said with embarrassment.

"I wish you were my sister, sister," said Raven.

"Starfire's gonna be *so* proud of you," Cyborg added.

Whaaaaaam!

The living room shook violently as a giant hole suddenly erupted in a wall. Starfire came crashing into the room and landed with a thud next to the Titans.

"Hey, Starfire is back!" Beast Boy yelled happily.

"Dude, that girl is buff!" Cyborg observed.

"Um, Star?" Robin said nervously.

Pow!

Starfire slammed her fist into Robin's gut, sending him crashing against a wall.

43

"Robin!" cried out Beast Boy in alarm.

Starfire pointed her finger at Blackfire and said, "I am here for her!"

As Starfire started walking threateningly toward her sister, Robin called out, "Blackfire, remember your lessons! It's the only way to save yourself…and your relationship!"

"Starfire, sweetie…" said Blackfire.

Zzzap!

Starfire blasted her sister with a starbolt, but Blackfire jumped out of the way.

"You have never done anything for me, except use me and trick me and get me in trouble!" Starfire yelled.

"I hear you, and I'm sorry!" Blackfire said soothingly as she dodged Starfire's massive energy blasts.

"It is too late for the sorry!" screamed Starfire.

"You look like you could use a hug," offered Blackfire.

"Arrrrrgh!" yelled Starfire with rage as she lunged for her sister and knocked Blackfire through the hole in the wall. The sisters went flying through the air, soaring far away from Titans Tower. Starfire's hands were tightly clasped around Blackfire's throat as they careened through downtown Jump City, crashing through building after building.

Blam! Blam! Blam!

One skyscraper window after another shattered into tiny shards of glass as the pair zoomed through the city. Starfire was still clutching Blackfire's throat.

Crash!

The sisters smashed through the window of a clothing store, knocking over mannequins and displays. Blackfire spotted a purple dress in the wreckage of the store and quickly reached for it.

"This would look great on you," she said as

she held the dress in the air.

Zaaap!

Starfire blasted the dress to shreds with an eye blast.

"I am not falling for the act again!" Starfire roared as she raised her fists in the air and prepared to pummel her sister.

Blackfire reached into her pocket and said, "Wait, I've got something to show you."

Starfire's eyes widened in surprise as her sister removed a small doll from her pocket and held it up in the air. It was Tina Tinkles, the very same doll that Blackfire had stolen from her years ago.

Starfire's frown melted away, and tears glistened in both her eyes.

"The dolly you stole from me as a child? Where did you get it?"

47

"I've had it the whole time," Blackfire said sadly. "I shouldn't have taken it, and I shouldn't have kept it. I'm sorry."

Starfire reached out a trembling hand and took the doll from her sister. She held it up to her cheek for a moment, and then she smiled at Blackfire.

"You really *have* changed?" Starfire asked.

"Yes, I have," Blackfire said happily as she reached out her arms to hug her sister.

"Well, so have I," said Starfire as she took a step closer to her sister and extended her left arm to draw Blackfire closer.

Starfire then punched Blackfire so hard that her sister went flying through the air and disappeared from sight.

"I am so glad that we were able to work things out, sister," said Starfire with a grin as she flexed her bicep.

TAMARANIAN VACATION

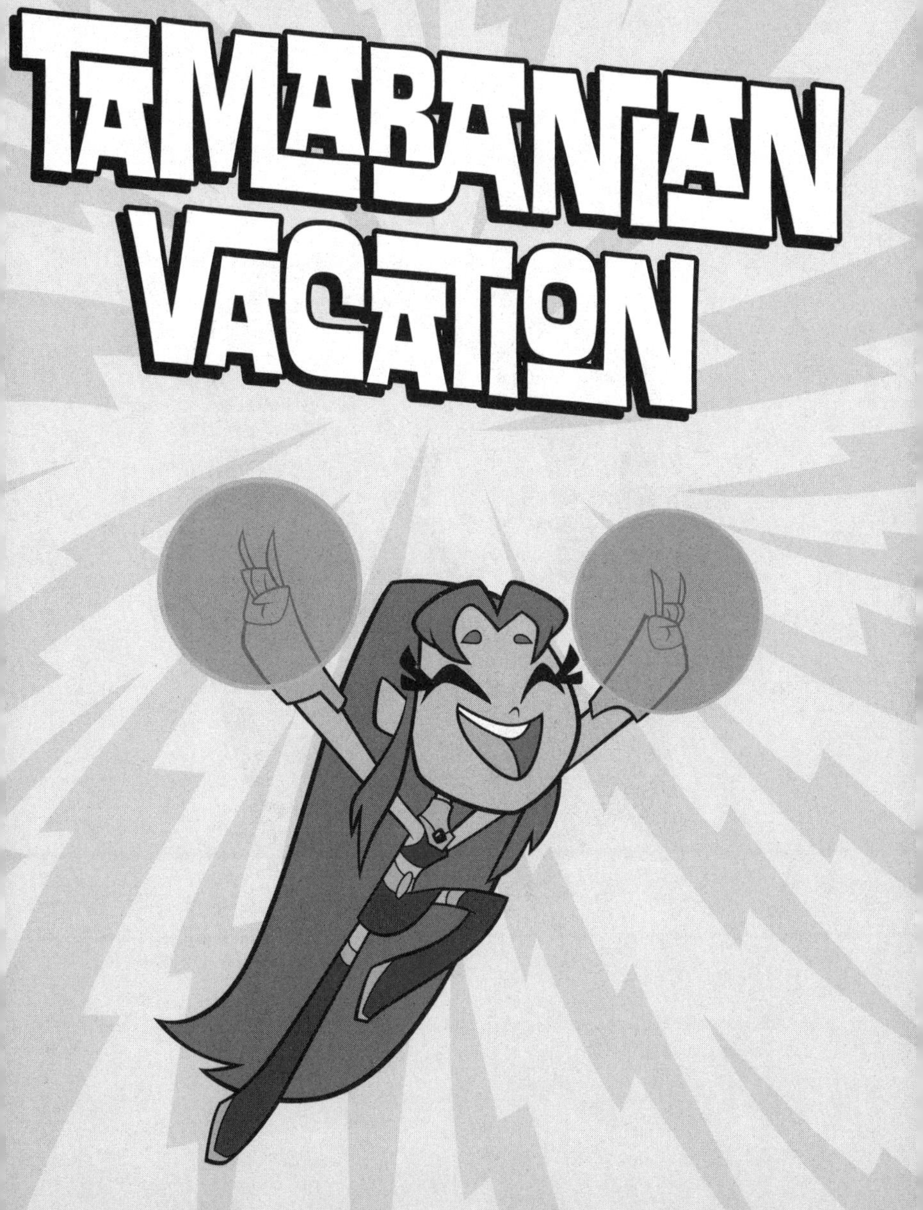

CHAPTER 1

"Please, Starfire! You don't have to do this!"

It was far from an ordinary day in the living room of Titans Tower. Robin was down on his knees, pleading for mercy from Starfire, who hovered in the air above him. The other Titans cowered in the corner, watching as Starfire raised her hand menacingly and shouted at Robin in a harsh, metallic tone that was the opposite of her usual cheerful voice. Her normally bright eyes were two glowing green orbs.

"I *must* do this," she bellowed. "Accept your fate, human, and I will end it quickly!"

"Never!" shouted Robin as he jumped to his feet and assumed his fighting pose.

Starfire's face darkened as she said, "Very well. Remember that you asked for this...."

Suddenly, the green glow disappeared from her eyes, and a wide smile spread across her lips. Starfire wiggled her fingers and shouted happily, "It is time for the *Tickle War!*"

"Titans, GO!" Robin said with a laugh as the other four Titans assumed defensive poses.

Starfire swooped through the air in pursuit of Beast Boy, who transformed himself into a green gazelle and loped across the living room. Soon, he was trapped in the corner.

Starfire raced after him, her fingers moving quickly over his green fur and tickling the bottoms of his hooves.

"No...don't!" wailed Beast Boy as he fell on the floor and giggled uncontrollably. "Please...stop....I gotta pee!"

Starfire smiled in triumph, and she flew across the room toward Cyborg.

"It's no use, Star," he said smugly. "My computer parts can't be tickled."

"Oh, really?" Starfire said as she reached

forward to push a button on his chest armor. With a snap, a panel opened at the front of Cyborg's stomach, and a bit of his human belly popped out. Starfire moved in to tickle his exposed stomach.

"No…not…the…belly…button!" Cyborg cried out, guffawing loudly.

Raven assumed a defensive stance, hiding deep within her blue cloak. Starfire channeled all her happy energy to break through Raven's dark forces and tickled her teammate for a few seconds.

"Hee-hee, got me," admitted Raven as she emitted a nanosecond of laughter.

Starfire then turned to Robin, who was crouched in his fiercest fighting stance and clasping his staff in his hands.

"It's just us now," declared Robin.

"Your tummy will not survive my tickling fingers, Robin," warned Starfire.

She zoomed toward Robin, but he did a quick backflip and knocked Starfire off course with a kick. She turned around and extended her fingers until they touched Robin's stomach. Robin doubled over in laughter as she expertly tickled him.

"Enough…enough.…You win!" he cried out as he squirmed on the floor.

"As Cyborg would say, the *booyah*!" said a triumphant Starfire.

She then turned to her pet, a mutant moth larva named Silkie, who had been sitting on the couch. Silkie quickly rolled over and exposed his tiny pink tummy.

"And I couldn't forget *you*, my little *bumgorf*," Starfire said as she ran her fingers over Silkie's stomach. The little creature giggled happily.

The other Titans smiled as Starfire played with Silkie.

"Man, Starfire is *so* upbeat," observed Cyborg.

"Her happiness makes *me* happy," added Robin.

Beast Boy turned to Raven and said, "The longest *you* were ever in a good mood was *three seconds*."

Raven frowned and then slammed her fist into Beast Boy's head, knocking him across the room.

"Owwwwwww!" wailed Beast Boy.

Starfire floated above her teammates and asked, "Who is ready for the Tickle War, Part Two?"

"I have to know, Star," said Cyborg. "Just where does your cheery disposition come from?"

Starfire pondered the question, and then she said, "I suppose it comes from growing up on my home planet, Tamaran."

"If it made you this nice, it must be the best place in the universe," said Robin as he dreamily closed his eyes and imagined a planet filled with hundreds and hundreds of Starfires, all lined up in a row, waiting to plant a kiss on his lips.

"Mwwwah! Mwwwah! Mwwwah!" he said quietly as he puckered his lips and imagined each smooch with another Starfire.

The other Titans glanced at Robin nervously, wondering what was wrong with him.

"Star, when are you going to take us there?" asked Beast Boy.

Starfire hesitated for a moment before she

responded. "Oh, I am not sure you would like it."

"We like *you*," said Raven. "I'm sure we will like your planet."

"You may find my Tamaranian ways strange, much like I find some of the Earth ways strange," said Starfire. "But it would mean so much to me if I could share this special place with you."

Beast Boy jumped up in the air and popped a space helmet on top of his head.

"Then share away!" he yelled. "Let's go to space!"

CHAPTER 2

VROOOOOOM!

Titans Tower, which was doubling as the team's super-fast rocket ship, launched with a mighty roar into outer space. Two hours later, in defiance of every law of physics, the ship entered the outer atmosphere of the planet Tamaran.

After the Tower slowly descended to the ground, Starfire was the first to exit the ship.

She inhaled a deep breath and clasped her hands together in delight.

"Oh, it is so good to be home. I missed the crispness of Tamaranian air."

The other four Titans stepped out of the Tower and took deep breaths.

"Aaaaaack!" they all yelled as a deep, burning pain erupted in each of their lungs. They frantically waved their hands and wailed in pain.

"My lungs are crying!" screamed Robin.

"What are we breathing, Star?" demanded Cyborg.

"That is the Tamaranian Fire Air," Starfire said happily.

"What?! Your planet's air is made out of hot sauce?!" yelled Beast Boy.

"It ensures the weak do not survive," Starfire said calmly. "You will grow accustomed to the burning."

"The pain! The pain!" cried Cyborg, spitting out a stream of hot red flames.

Starfire looked on with sympathy as her teammates collapsed to the ground, streams of fire bursting from their mouths.

"Oh, do not die so quickly, friends," she said warmly. "We have just arrived, and there are so many more wonderful things to see."

Starfire and her four guests continued their journey to the capital city of Tamaran, where an ornate, gold-plated castle towered over every other building. Starfire smiled as she led the other Titans into the palace.

"Give us the tour, Star," said Beast Boy. "We want to see all the things that made you such a sweet cuddle bug."

"This place is amazing!" said Robin as they walked through the richly decorated rooms of the palace. Within each room, an assortment of aliens and intergalactic creatures of every species craned their necks to stare at the Titans.

"As a Tamaranian princess, this palace was my home," said Starfire. "We often entertained kings, queens, and warlords in an effort to keep the peace of the galaxy."

Just then, a large slimy green alien slithered into the room. It wore a heavy metal helmet atop its head. Below its two giant eyes were over two dozen long tentacles, and at the end of each tentacle was a pulsating mouth. As it approached the Titans, each of its mouths slowly opened and closed, displaying dozens of razor-sharp teeth.

Then six smaller slimy aliens entered the room and stood behind the larger one.

"Eeeeew," said Beast Boy nervously.

"This is General Thraxxes of the Blood Dominion," Starfire said proudly. "We are working on an important treaty with him right now."

Cyborg stepped forward, grabbed one of General Thraxxes's tentacles, and shook it.

67

"What up, General?" Cyborg said with an eager smile.

Blorrrrrrt!

General Thraxxes let out a cry of rage and yanked the tentacle from Cyborg's hand. The six smaller aliens quickly encircled their leader and, glaring at the Teen Titans, led the general from the room.

"What was *that* about?" asked Robin.

"On Tamaran, a handshake is the most violent declaration of war," Starfire explained. "General Thraxxes has vowed to wipe out my people and turn Tamaran into intergalactic gravel."

"My bad," Cyborg said quietly.

"That is the all right," Starfire replied. "But you must excuse me. I need to rally a planetary defense. You may watch the invasion from

68

the terrace. Help yourself to anything in the kitchen."

"Star...wait...*what*?!" Robin said.

Starfire had already grabbed a giant sword off the wall and was rushing out of the palace.

CHAPTER 3

"**Chaaaaaarge!**" **yelled Starfire as she** held her sword aloft and floated high above the palace. Surrounding her were fifty Tamaranian troops, each soldier wearing a suit of armor and brandishing a heavy sword. The Tamaranian forces zoomed into the air, where they were met by fifty Blood Dominion hovercrafts. General Thraxxes was riding atop the first ship, his many mouths angrily opening and closing.

Zzzzap! Voooom! Krakoww!

One of the Blood Dominion ships shot a laser beam at the Tamaranians. In return, a Tamaranian soldier fired an energy blast at a Blood Dominion fighter.

Down below, on the palace's terrace, the four Teen Titans nervously watched the unfolding war.

"Do you *have* to shake everyone's hand?" Robin said to Cyborg.

"I'm a friendly guy—what can I do?!"

Cyborg said.

"This is *not* what I was expecting," Raven said. "I'm not sure I like Starfire's planet."

"It's definitely not as sweet as she is," agreed Cyborg.

"True," added Beast Boy. "But it's pretty cool watching those green alien guys explode. There goes one now!"

Sure enough, a Tamaranian energy ray blasted into a Blood Dominion fighter, blowing it into bits and sending blobs of green goo plummeting toward the palace.

Splat!

Each Titan was drenched with globs of steaming hot green slime. They fell to the ground, wailing in pain.

"Oooooow! My face!" Robin screamed.

"It hurts! It hurts!" yelled Beast Boy.

"Why does everything *burn* on this planet?"

"This is terrible," said Raven as she scraped the green goo off her cloak. "Let's get out of here before things get worse."

"No, Raven, we can't," said Robin. "It means so much to Starfire that we're here."

Beast Boy suddenly pointed to the sky and said, "Yo! The cries of terror have stopped!"

The Titans paused to listen for a moment. There was silence.

"Maybe Cyborg's Handshake War is over," said Robin.

"Handshakes are *friendly*," Cyborg said defensively. "I don't care who you are.... They're *friendly*!"

Suddenly, Starfire floated into view. Her hair was disheveled and her outfit was torn, but she smiled.

"Good news, friends," she said. "The war has concluded. And only three-quarters of the planet was destroyed!"

Robin forced a smile and said, "That's great, Star. I'm so happy for you."

"As is the custom on Tamaran, I brokered a truce by offering my hand in marriage to General Thraxxes," Starfire added.

Robin's eyes widened, his mouth fell open, and he started wailing, "Nooooooooooo!"

As the other Titans looked on in amazement, Robin suddenly pounced on top of Cyborg and started throwing wild punches at his teammate.

"*Why* did you have to shake his hand?!" Robin screamed. "*Why*?!"

Cyborg grabbed Robin by the hair and held him at arm's length as he explained again,

"I told you. I'm a friendly guy. I like to put people at ease."

Robin continued to flail his arms in the air, sobbing loudly.

CHAPTER 4

In a small chapel near the palace, the soft sounds of an organ drifted through the Tamaranian air. The only other sound to be heard was the quiet sobbing of Robin, who was sitting in a pew next to the other Titans. They watched as Starfire exchanged her wedding vows with the many-mouthed alien General Thraxxes.

"That should have been *me*," Robin pouted.

"I really, really, *really* hate this planet. How can anyone as nice and perfect as Starfire come from here?"

As the ceremony ended, and Starfire labored to shove a wedding ring onto one of the general's stubby fingers, Robin sobbed even louder.

"Ewww, look!" said Beast Boy. "Now that they're married, she has to kiss all those gross mouths."

"Mwwwah! Mwwwah! Mwwwah!" Starfire's lips connected with one mouth after another on her husband's now happy face.

Cyborg turned to Robin with sympathy and said, "And she never kissed you on your one mouth. Bummer."

"We're going to be here a while," Raven muttered. "He has a *lot* of mouths."

Two dozen slimy kisses later, Starfire turned to face her friends and said, "Was the ceremony not beautiful? Now, please enjoy the rest of your stay on Tamaran. I must go."

"Where are you going, Star?" asked Beast Boy sadly.

"As the general's wife, I must travel with his fleet as he conquers the universe," she replied. "You will never see me again."

"What? You can't go with him," said Raven.

"I know our customs seem strange, but it is important to honor them," replied Starfire. "Good-bye forever, friends."

As Starfire turned to take hold of one of her husband's tentacles, Cyborg jumped to his feet and yelled, "This is *not* cool!"

Robin stood up and declared, "If Starfire is going to be forced to marry anyone, it's going to be me!"

Raven and Beast Boy gathered next to their teammates as Robin cried out, "Titans, let's *annul* this marriage!"

Brandishing his staff, Robin jumped into the air and quickly extracted three exploding Batarangs from his utility belt.

Whoosh! Whoosh! Whoosh!

Robin launched the three Batarangs into the air and watched with satisfaction as they expertly soared into three open mouths on the startled face of General Thraxxes.

Ker-Splat!

Globs of hot green slime splattered over the entire chapel, covering the Teen Titans and most of the wedding guests.

As the Titans wailed in pain from the hot goo, Starfire asked in confusion, "Friends, why did you blow up my husband? The peace treaty is now broken. The general's army will soon attack, and I have dishonored my people."

"And you are *welcome*!" Robin yelled angrily. "He was gross!"

As Raven wiped more slime off her cloak, she agreed, "Super gross."

Starfire paused to think for a moment, and then she said, "Now the only way to save my planet from the invasion is in a traditional show of bravery by fighting Gridnock the Skull Crusher."

"And if you don't, this planet will be destroyed?" asked Cyborg.

"Yes," said Starfire.

"Sounds good to me!" yelled Beast Boy.

Before the Titans could move, they were

surrounded by an army of Tamaranian guards. They all carried giant axes, the sharp edges of each blade glinting in the light.

"These are the Guardians of Honor," said Starfire. "They will escort us to our inevitable death at the hands of Gridnock. Hello, Guardians. Keeping those axes sharp, I see!"

CHAPTER 5

Far beneath the palace, in a dark and dank dungeon, the five Teen Titans huddled together, shivering in the cold.

Clang!

The iron door at the end of the dungeon was opened. Beyond the door, the Titans saw a large stadium and heard the cheering crowds anxious to view the battle between them and Gridnock the Skull Crusher.

"Wait until you see Gridnock," Starfire said happily to her teammates. They slowly emerged from the dungeon and entered the dusty arena, their eyes blinking in the bright sunlight.

The crowd's cheers grew even louder as the Titans walked to the middle of the arena.

Roaaaaaaar!

Suddenly, an ear-piercing growl filled the air as an iron door at the other end of the stadium was flung open.

The eyes of the Teen Titans grew wider as an enormous monster, over one hundred feet tall and covered in leathery orange scales, stomped to the middle of the arena and opened its giant mouth.

"Is he not magnificent?" asked Starfire.

"Why are you so happy about this?" asked Raven.

"It is an honor to prove one's bravery on Tamaran," explained Starfire.

"So...how many people have survived

Gridnock?" asked Beast Boy nervously as he viewed the scattered piles of broken skeletons that had been shoved to the edge of the arena.

"None," said Starfire. "That is why it is such an *honor*!"

"None?" said Robin as he crouched into a fighting stance. "Well, Gridnock has never faced the Teen Titans. TITANS, GO!"

With a joyous battle cry, the Teen Titans bravely charged toward Gridnock...

Gulp!

...and Gridnock immediately swallowed all five Titans.

CHAPTER 6

Deep within the stomach of Gridnock the Skull Crusher, the five Titans were huddled together on a small island of half-digested food parts in the middle of a pool of Gridnock's boiling hot stomach acid.

"Whoa! Did we just get eaten?" asked Cyborg. "That was *fast*!"

As the stomach acid started to rise up closer to their island, Robin said, "Don't take this the wrong way, Star, but we hate your planet and everything on it."

Starfire looked sad and said, "You are hurting the feelings, Robin."

"It's true," said Raven. "This planet is awful."

"We have no idea how *you* came from a place like this!" added Beast Boy.

"Yes, life can be hard on Tamaran," admitted Starfire, "but if I only saw the negative, my skull would have been crushed many years ago. Instead, I have learned to find the best in any situation. In fact, that is the only way I have been able to tolerate you all as my roommates."

Beast Boy wiped a tear from his eye and said, "Oh, Star, that's beautiful. I always wondered why you didn't hate us."

Rrrrrumble!

The island below the Titans wavered as Gridnock's stomach acid continued to rise.

"Well, if we're all going to die, we might as well be positive like Starfire," said Cyborg.

"We're in an alien monster's belly," Raven said with a nod. "What's not to love?"

Cyborg reached his hand into the acid and extracted a ragged chunk of mystery meat.

"Oh, look!" he said happily. "Is that a half-eaten hot dog?" He popped the discovery into his mouth.

Blooork!

Seconds later, after Cyborg vomited over the side of the island, he smiled bravely and said, "Nope, not a hot dog. But I've never tasted anything like it. Very salty!"

Beast Boy dangled his feet over the edge

of the island and dipped his boots into the stomach acid.

"It's so nice and warm in here," said Beast Boy as the acid ate away at his boots. "Like a free sauna!"

Buuuurp!

A loud belch from Gridnock knocked the Titans off their feet, and their island sank a few inches deeper into the boiling hot liquid below them.

Just then, Robin had an idea.

"If Star only survived on this planet because of her positive attitude, then we have to think like her. You know what that means...."

He paused dramatically as his teammates looked on, and then he shouted, "Titans, Tickle War!"

CHAPTER

7

And so began the Titans' epic Tickle War deep within the stomach of Gridnock the Skull Crusher.

Starfire moved quickly to Cyborg's chest armor and popped open the panel that covered his ample stomach. Starfire began to tickle his exposed belly.

"Belly button! Whooo! Whooo! *Whooo!*" cried Cyborg with helpless laughter as he catapulted up and crashed into the inner lining of Gridnock's stomach. Still laughing hysterically, Cyborg bounced from one side of the monster's stomach to another. With each collision, Cyborg knocked another hole in Gridnock's abdomen.

"If Cyborg knocks enough holes in Gridnock's stomach," Robin said, "then maybe he will…"

Ker-Blam!

Before Robin could finish his sentence, Gridnock exploded into thousands of tiny orange fragments. The battered Titans tumbled to the floor of the arena.

"We defeated the Gridnock!" exclaimed Starfire.

Robin smiled at Starfire and said, "We couldn't have done it without seeing things the Tamaranian way, Star."

"Now you understand why I love this planet so?" asked Starfire.

"I think we do, Star," said Raven.

"Then perhaps you will let me show you *more* of Tamaran?" offered Starfire.

The other four Titans jumped back in horror.

"Are you *crazy*?!" yelled Cyborg.

"Let's get *out* of here," said Raven.

"Worst planet *ever*!" declared Beast Boy as the Titans sprinted back to their ship.

KNOWLEDGE

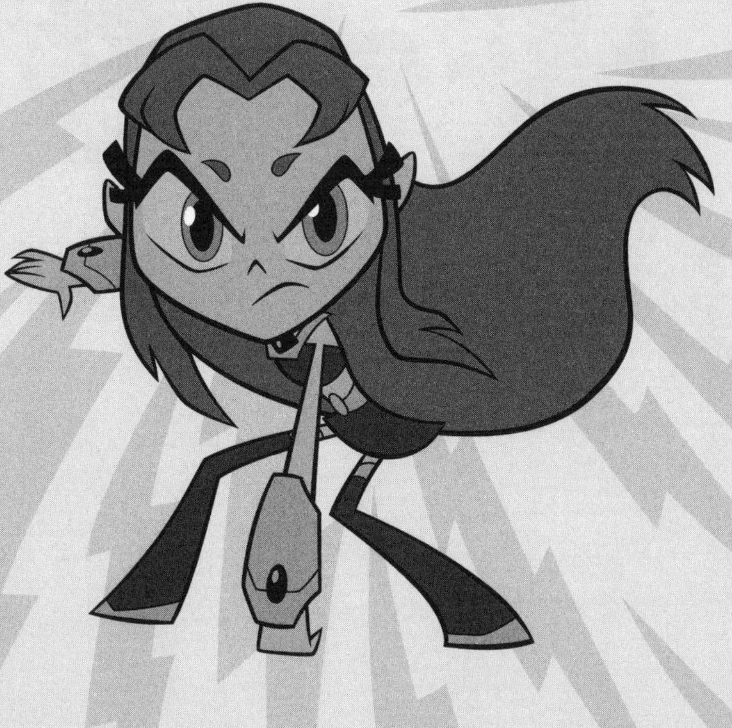

CHAPTER 1

"This is *very* important, Titans," Robin said loudly as he removed a thermometer and an expandable telescope from his utility belt, then waved them with a flourish in the air.

He had gathered the Teen Titans together in the living room of Titans Tower. Sunshine poured through the windows as Cyborg, Raven, Beast Boy, and Starfire waited patiently for Robin to get to the point.

"Temperature at eighty-two degrees," Robin said as he studied the thermometer. "Winds gusting from a southwestwardly direction at ten knots."

He unfolded the telescope, pressed it against the window, and peered into the distance.

"Clear skies and bright sun," he said. "Really bright. Really, *really* bright. It's happening, Titans."

His teammates looked at one another questioningly. What did this mean?

Robin took a deep breath, leaned closer, and whispered, "Yes, it's all there, Titans. The conditions are perfect for a…"

Robin paused dramatically for a moment, and then he shouted, "…beach day!"

"*Yaaaaay*!" The other Titans erupted into excited cheers.

"Sand castles!" yelled Cyborg.

"Surfing!" shouted Beast Boy.

"Water," observed Raven calmly.

"Seashells!" said Starfire with a smile.

Then, without warning, Starfire opened her mouth and yawned. Her horrified teammates looked on in disbelief.

"Star, did you just *yawn*?!" Robin asked in a panicky voice.

"Excuse me," she said. "I did not sleep very well."

"Quarantine! Quarantine!" shouted Robin as he ran to a control panel at the far end of the room. He frantically pounded a button on the panel.

Whooosh!

A thick, Plexiglas column descended from

the ceiling and quickly encased Starfire within its transparent wall.

"What did I do?" Starfire asked with puzzlement.

"You yawned!" declared Cyborg.

"Don't you know that yawns are contagious?" said Beast Boy sternly.

"I have never heard that," admitted Starfire.

"Well, it's a very well-known fun fact! Don't you pay attention to pointless trivia?" asked Cyborg.

Starfire pushed her hands against the Plexiglas and asked, "What do the yawns transmit?"

"*Sleep*! They transmit *sleep*!" bellowed Beast Boy.

Robin moved closer to his teammates and tried to restore order.

"It's okay," he said. "I think we caught it in time. Beach day is still a go."

"That was close," Beast Boy said with a sigh…and a yawn.

Beast Boy quickly clapped his hands over his mouth, hoping that his teammates hadn't seen his yawn.

"Beast Boy! Not you, too!" said Cyborg.

"It's…it's not what you think!" Beast Boy said quickly. "I wasn't yawning—I was…I was just breathing weird! Let's hit the beach, fools, c'mon!"

Robin's hand hovered near the control panel, and he said, "I'm sorry, old friend. It has to be this way."

Whooosh!

A second Plexiglas tube slammed to the ground, surrounding Beast Boy. Within seconds, he was curled up on the floor and sleeping peacefully.

Cyborg peered into Beast Boy's transparent prison and said, "I'll never forget you, buddy."

And then Cyborg yawned.

Whooosh!

"Aw, man," Cyborg moaned as he slowly drifted into sleep inside his Plexiglas tube.

Robin turned to his one remaining teammate and said, "Well, Raven, it looks like it's just you and... *Wait!*... Was that a *yawn*?!"

Raven quickly shut her half-open mouth and said guiltily, "No."

She paused for a moment, sighed, then admitted, "Yes."

Whooosh!

Seconds later, Robin was the only Titan

not encased in Plexiglas. He pounded his fists together and declared, "These naps will not be taken in vain. I vow to make the most of this perfect beach day!"

His eyes began to close, and he fought to stifle the yawn that was starting to form around his lips.

"Must...not...yawn...." he protested. "Must...show...off...hot...beach...bod.... *Yawn*!"

Whooosh!

The final Plexiglas column covered Robin.

CHAPTER 2

It was ten o'clock that night when the Teen Titans began to stir from their naps. Robin was the first to fully awaken, and he let out a scream when he looked at his wristwatch.

"Eeek! We slept through the most perfect beach day we'll see for the next…!" he wailed as he peered at a small digital device he had extracted from his utility belt. He concluded sadly, "…for the next twenty-four years!"

"I am sorry, fellow Titans," said Starfire. "I did not know about the yawns!"

Cyborg shrugged and said, "It's all right, Star, no big."

"No, friend Cyborg," argued Starfire. "It is the 'all wrong.' This is not the first time my ignorance of Earth culture has ruined the merriment. Remember when I attacked those two small Earth children who arrived on Halloween because I thought they were the villainous Slade and a tiger wearing suspenders?" Starfire hung her head in shame. "I will forever be the celebration ruiner."

"The term is *party pooper*, Star," offered Beast Boy.

Starfire gasped and said, "I have never done such a thing to a party!"

"Star, we love you just the way you are," said Robin.

"And the more you knew, the bigger bummer you would become," said Beast Boy.

"That's right," agreed Cyborg. "Like Raven."

"I am *not* a bummer," insisted Raven.

"You're a total bummer, Raven," Robin said as he set up an easel and placed a large piece of paper on it. "If you will look at these charts, you will see that there is a direct correlation between knowledge and being a bummer. For example, take Beast Boy and Cyborg. Together, they know virtually nothing, and everybody loves them!"

"Thanks, man!" said Beast Boy.

Robin pointed to another graphic. "And here's my chart. I don't know too much or too little, leaving people not feeling very strongly about me one way or another."

Robin then pointed to Raven's chart and said, "And here's you, Raven. You know a lot, and you bum everyone out."

Starfire studied the charts and said sadly, "I do not wish to be the bummer!"

Raven grunted her disapproval and floated out of the room.

Later that day, Raven was floating down the hallway when she heard Starfire crying in her bedroom.

"Are you okay, Star?" asked Raven as she slowly entered Starfire's room.

"It has happened again...." Starfire said between sobs.

"What happened?" asked Raven.

"A misunderstanding. Beast Boy asked me to set him up on the blind date...."

Just then, Beast Boy staggered into the room, his hands covering his eyes.

"Aaaaaaack! Why did you blast my eyes? I can't *see*!" he cried out as he ran in circles and then stumbled out of the room.

"I am the sorry…and the hopeless," Starfire called out as she softly whimpered.

"I'll take care of Beast Boy's eyes," said Raven. "And I can help you, too. Do you want me to teach you some stuff?"

"But will that make me the bummer?" asked Starfire.

"No way!" said Raven. "Knowledge is power. I'll give you a crash course in all things Earth-related."

"I would prefer a course without any crashing."

Raven rolled her eyes and continued. "Which brings me to lesson one: common expressions. You don't have to take everything so literally. Sometimes people say things with a little style."

"Oooh, interesting," Starfire said. "I do not understand."

"Hmmm, how can I make you understand?" pondered Raven.

"Perhaps through song?" Starfire asked.

"Ugh, fine," Raven said reluctantly as she magically produced a piano and reached for a microphone. Seconds later, she was crooning a song for Starfire.

> *Don't say what you mean,*
> *But mean what you say.*
> *It sounds complicated, but*
> *It's easy in every way.*

Starfire danced around the room as Raven continued her song.

> *Don't say you're going to sleep. Nuh-uh.*
> *Instead you're catching zzzs.*
> *Never say that things were easy.*
> *No. Just say that they were a breeze.*
> *Don't say watch how you spend,*
> *Say money don't grow on trees.*
> *You say what you gotta say every day,*
> *But say it with style, and you'll do okay.*

"Got it?" Raven asked as she made the piano disappear.

Starfire clapped her hands together with delight and said, "I believe I understand! Your song was so kitten!"

"Kitten?" asked Raven.

"Yes! Kittens are good," explained Starfire. "And so your song was good. Wait, am I not meaning what I say?"

Raven sighed and said, "Ugh. Clearly a song is not going to do it."

Starfire threw herself back onto her bed and started crying into her pillow.

"It is the okay," she said between sobs. "My ignorance will always hold me back."

Raven pondered for a moment and then snapped her fingers.

"I've got it!" she said. "Lesson number two:

115

time for a little magic."

Raven closed her eyes to concentrate and slowly began to chant a magic spell.

"Azarath Metrion Zinthos!" she intoned.

Pooof!

A purple medallion appeared in her hand.

"Sleep with this tonight, and in the morning you'll know everything," Raven said, handing the magical relic to Starfire.

"Oh, thank you!" said Starfire as she reached out to hug her teammate.

"Ugh. No hugging," said Raven.

CHAPTER 3

The next morning found Beast Boy, Cyborg, Starfire, and Raven gathered around the kitchen table, eating cereal for breakfast.

Robin entered the room and said, "So I checked the weather, and today has all the perfect conditions for a…"

He paused, and then he yelled, "…lake day!"

"Jet Skis!" said Beast Boy.

"Fishing," added Cyborg.

"Water," observed Raven calmly.

"Pollution," added Starfire.

The other Titans stared at Starfire in disbelief.

"It is true," Starfire said. "Forty-six percent of lakes are too polluted for recreational activities."

"Why are we talking about numbers on lake day?" grumbled Beast Boy.

"Because numbers reveal undeniable facts," explained Starfire. "Like slightly over one trillion gallons of sewage are dumped into lakes each year."

"Robin, make her *stop*!" bellowed Cyborg. "These facts are bumming me out!"

"Sewage...*yuck*!" said Beast Boy.

"Starfire, what's gotten into you?" demanded Robin.

"Knowledge, that's what," she replied. "Did you know that seven hundred species of bacteria thrive in the average human mouth?"

"That is so gross!" cried Cyborg.

"These numbers are bumming me out!" yelled Beast Boy.

"I think it's kinda interesting," Raven added.

Robin turned to glare at Raven and said, "Did *you* have something to do with this, Raven?"

"I *may* have magically given her all human knowledge," Raven said, and then she added defensively, "I was just trying to *help*!"

"That is what I wanted, Robin," said Starfire. "Now you won't have to deal with me ruining another occasion."

"You just ruined lake day!" screamed Robin.

"Knowledge is power, Robin," explained Raven. "This will only make her stronger."

"Or…a total bummer," said Cyborg.

Later that morning, Raven looked up from the book she was reading to see that Starfire was staring at her.

"That book is so overrated," Starfire said smugly. "I'll save you some time. Everyone dies in the end."

"Bummer," Raven said with a grunt as she dumped the book into a garbage can.

After lunch, Raven was quietly meditating in her bedroom. Her eyes were closed, and she floated six inches above her bed.

Starfire poked her head into the room and said, "Meditation can cause problems ranging from muscle spasms to hallucinations."

Raven's eyes popped open, and she tumbled down to her bed.

"Bummer," she muttered.

Outside Titans Tower that afternoon, Raven hummed happily as she played with her *Pretty, Pretty Pegasus* toys.

Starfire floated by and pointed out, "You know that those toys are meant for babies, right?"

"Bummer!" Raven yelled as she tossed her toys across the lawn. "Aaaargh!"

CHAPTER

4

That evening, Raven called for a Titans meeting with Robin, Cyborg, and Beast Boy.

"Okay, you were right," Raven conceded. "Starfire is a total bummer now."

"There has to be a way to get the old Starfire back," said Robin.

"She's still there," Raven said, "but we have to go inside her mind and destroy all her knowledge."

"That sounds dangerous," Beast Boy said nervously.

"Extremely," agreed Raven. "Both for her and for us."

Starfire entered the room and asked, "Do you guys want to know where hot dog meat comes from?"

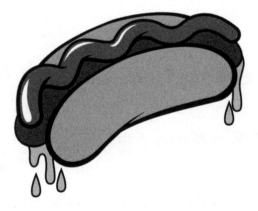

"No, I *don't*!" yelled Cyborg with alarm. "I do *not* want to! Raven, let's *do* this!"

"Azarath Metrion Zinthos!" Raven chanted, casting another magical spell.

Instantly, the four Titans were shrunk down and crammed into a microscopic submarine that floated into Starfire's ear. Soon, the craft was navigating its way through the Starfire's bloodstream. Small nuggets of information constantly pelted the craft, knocking the Titans off balance.

"Whoa, look at all that knowledge," Beast Boy said as he peered through the vehicle's windshield.

"This place is crawling with depressing

information," Robin observed. "Titans, stay alert!"

"Robin, fun facts at three o'clock!" warned Cyborg.

A handful of fun facts attacked the side of the submarine, but Robin deftly changed course and headed toward Starfire's brain.

He turned to Raven and asked, "Are you sure the old Starfire is in here?"

Suddenly, a deafening, ominous voice filled the craft, causing the Titans to clutch their ears.

"I won't let you find her!" the voice bellowed.

"Starfire…is that you?" Beast Boy called out nervously.

"I am knowledge," shouted the voice. "And facts, figures, and trivia."

"So you're the one who made Starfire a bummer," said Cyborg.

"Yes, I am!" the voice said angrily. "And when I am finished, she will be one hundred percent bummer!"

The Titans looked through the windshield and gasped when they saw a giant mass of brainpower. It floated in front of them and made their ship vibrate when it spoke.

"It's unnatural, and it's growing at an alarming rate," said Raven.

"Then let's nuke some neurons!" Robin yelled as he slammed his hand against a button on the control panel. Six giant missiles exploded from the craft, heading directly toward the brain mass.

"Eighty-five percent of missiles never reach their intended target," the brain mass said with a laugh as it easily swatted the missiles out of their path.

"How did you know that?" Cyborg called out in alarm.

"Fire lasers!" shouted Robin as a laser cannon extended from the craft and blasted bright laser rays toward the brain mass. They bounced harmlessly off it.

"Lasers have not advanced enough yet to inflict any real damage," it said.

"She's using facts and figures to deflect our attacks," Robin said angrily. "Her knowledge is too powerful. We don't stand a chance!"

Raven turned to her teammates and said, "I've got it. The only way to fight knowledge is with ignorance."

Outside the ship, the brain mass laughed harshly.

"Ha-ha-ha! This is like shooting fish in a barrel!"

Raven yelled out, doing her best impression of Starfire, "But I do not see the fish or barrels anywhere."

The brain mass winced at Raven's comment and explained angrily, "It's an expression, fools! I mean that destroying you will be a piece of cake!"

Robin chimed in to say, "I like the cake!

May I have the strawberry flavor?"

"Arrrgh!" moaned the brain mass in pain.
"I'm just trying to put a little style into what
I say! Defeating you will be a breeze!"

"Breeze? Do you need the coat?" asked
Cyborg with a big smile on his face.

"Eeek! Eeek! Eeek!" cried out the brain mass as it quivered and started to shrink.

"It's working," said Raven. "Our ignorance is overwhelming it! Fire away, Robin!"

Robin's hand hovered over the energy ray button, and he called out to the brain mass, "I've got one last fact for *you*! The Titans win one hundred percent of the time!"

"Wait! Is that true?" wailed the brain mass.

Ker-Blam!

A blinding ray of energy crashed into the brain mass, zapping it into tiny bits.

Minutes later, the tiny submarine, now covered with gooey brain matter, sailed out of Starfire's ear and back into the Titans' living room.

Pooof!

After Raven magically restored the Titans to their normal sizes, they anxiously looked at Starfire.

"How do you feel, Star?" asked Robin.

Starfire blinked and held one hand to her forehead.

"I feel…" she began. "I feel as if a thousand *glinkglats* are dancing on my *glipnorb*!"

As soon as she said that, the magical pendant around her neck shattered into tiny pieces and fell to the floor.

"She's back!" shouted Cyborg happily.

"Oh yeah!" yelled Beast Boy as he high-fived Robin.

"I'm sorry, Star," said Raven. "I shouldn't have used magic to cure you of your ignorance. I should have taken the time to teach you

133

the old-fashioned way: with books...and calculators...and flow charts...and more books...and..."

"*Bummer!*" cried the other Titans.

Something funny is going on in Starfire's room.
Spot the differences and solve who's
behind the mystery!

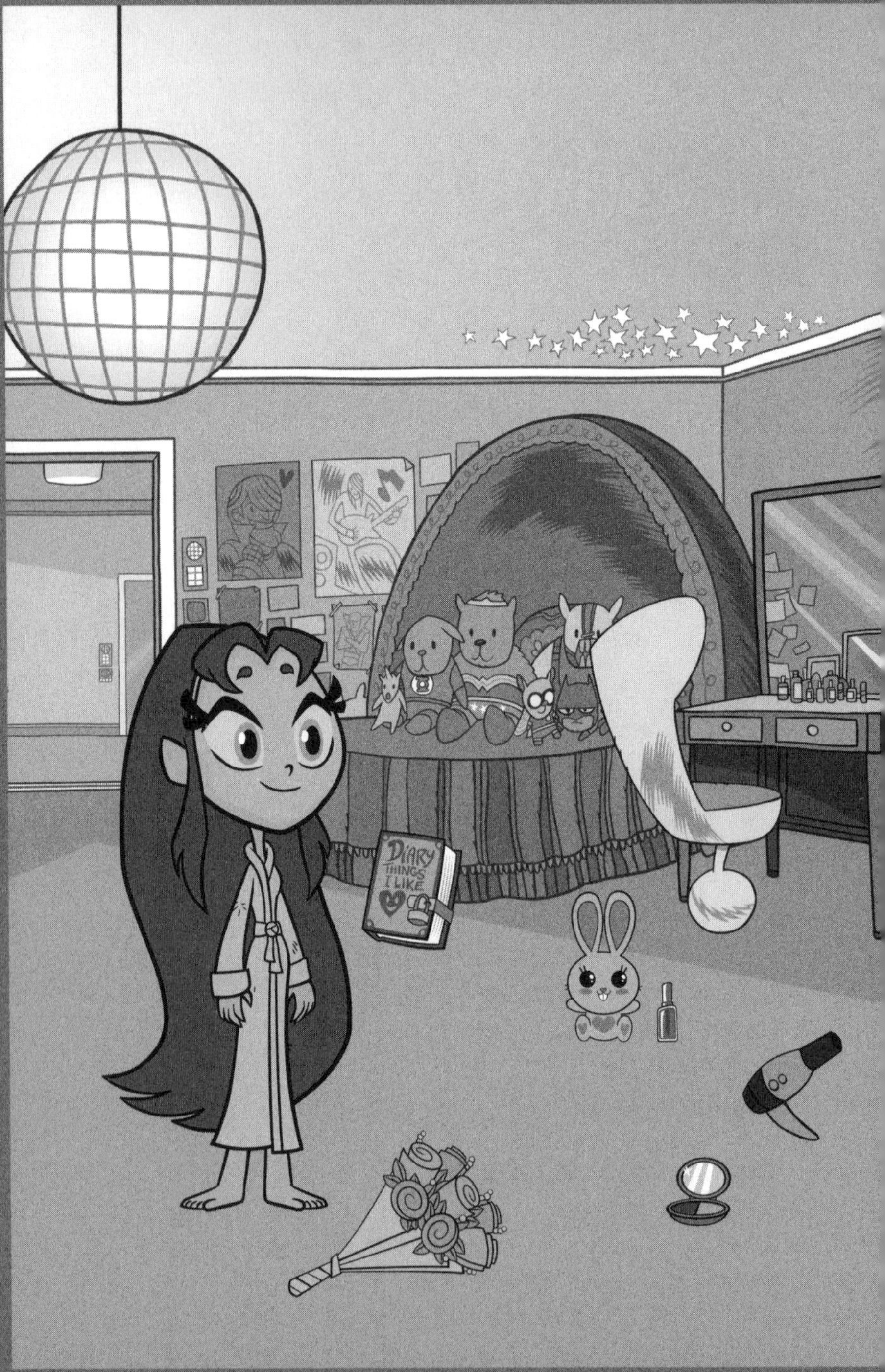
DIARY
THINGS I LIKE

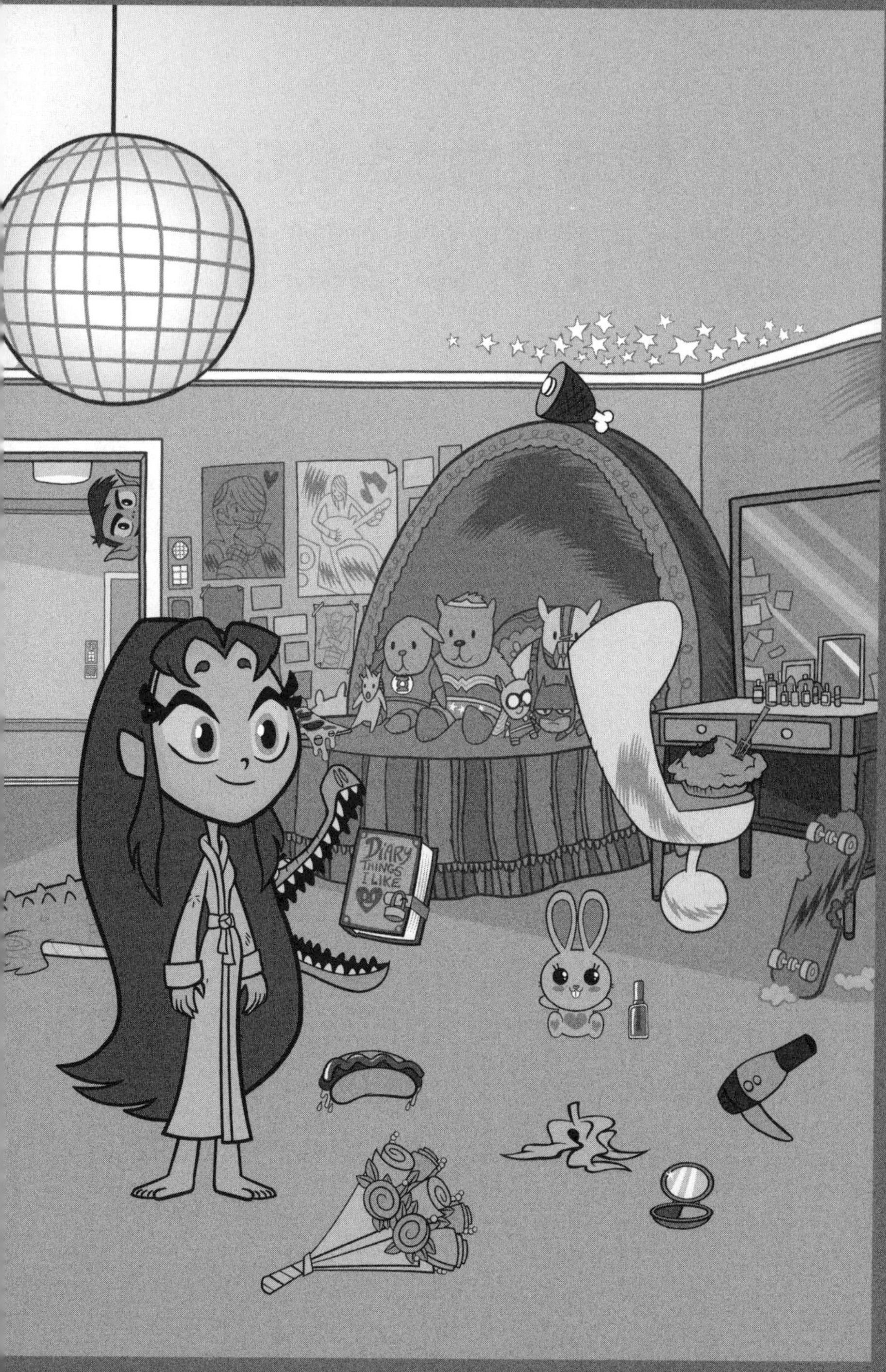
DIARY
THINGS
I LIKE

Don't miss these
TEEN TITANS GO! books.